The Soul Sentiments:

NO BLAMES FOR THIS PAIN

and other Selected Poems

With A Foreword And Introduction By:
MA. CARINA DIZON

Written by

EDISON DIZON

Philippine Copyright © 2021 by Edison Dizon

Published by Poetry Planet Book Publishing House
Designed by Micaella Dizon
Edited by Lyka Dizon
Compiled by Ma. Carina C. Dizon

Please submit all reviews and comments or report errors to edisondizon@hotmail.com
Photo used courtesy of Unsplash and may contain its own copywrites.

ISBN:

Hardbound- 978-621-8261-08-2

Softbound- 978-621-8261-07-5

Mobile/Kindle- 978-621-8261-09-9

FOREWORD

Edison Dizon is an educator, a very good writer, an artist, motivational speaker and an educational consultant. He is an author of several books and different journals and articles that were published in different countries worldwide. He is also a best-selling author and recently renowned as one of the greatest writer of his generation. He already holds a Master of Arts in Education and a Professional Degree in Higher Education Studies from Concordia University in Canada and currently working on his Doctorate, and now living a comfortable life in Angeles City with his family. Where he enjoys reading, travelling and writing at the same time.

He was my friend since college, He's one of my classmates in our major subject as we take the same course, Bachelor of Secondary Education Major in English, and I can't even imagine then that Edison will become a writer, although I know that he is really good in writing. He is also a person who will motivate and inspire you in your dreams in life.

Edison once told me that life is full of ups and downs, but all I need is to take one step forward and believe, just have faith in myself and have faith in God, learn to be positive that I can achieve all of my dreams in life.

His writing affects my life not only as a writer but as an author, knowing that in life we experience different seasons, different ideas though a positive or a negative side, and sometimes we may feel lonely, happy, sad, frustrated, we may even feel we are in love. His writing helps me a lot.

Love in life is when we learn to forgive and learn to accept whether it is good or bad. It is not how many times you see a person, not even how many times you kiss each other, hug each other; walk together holding hands but it is about that when you see each other and realize that you love each other. But when we talk about life, loving our life is appreciating all the things that we have and all people who motivates, inspires and love us.

The Soul Sentiments came out because of the request of the readers, to come up with a collection of poetry and the only reason I can say is, this compilation would change the life of his readers, who loves his works, who made them inspired on his previous book "Shades of Seasons Series" (Soulful Autumn, Cold Dark Winter's Night, Endless Spring and Summertime Blues) and the other one was "Isang Tasa ng Tsaa para Sa'yo: Tula at Prosa".

The theme was based on the authors' connotative meaning of each season, that we have different seasons in life that we experience; this compilation was so timely especially in this time of pandemic when we need something that will motivate and inspire us, and something to look forward.

The "Isang Tasa ng Tsaa para Sayo: Tula at Prosa" is a compilation of his work since he was 17-18 year of age; those were our college years, when he started writing poems and prose both in English and in Filipino.

This compilation, the author talks about the different sides of life, where in some of us we experience having a deadline or having bad experiences in life even to question our fate. At the end of the day, we will realize that we need to learn how to forgive and to accept things the way they are.

Keeping that anger in once heart may lead us into failure, we can say that life is so unfair, but death is a part of life, the author said it loud and clear that the unfairness of life and that new found appreciation, the time is too short for those who fear, and too long for those who grief. Yes, it is true but, Time is also valuable to us, for us to be able to see how beautiful life can be. For us to be able to heal ones heart and soul. Time is eternity.

In this book, we will also encounter the author saying that in love everything is pleasing our perfectly, but in loving someone you also need to accept and forgive the person who hurt you when you feel pain, the moment you love. And in the end, we should know our life purpose, know our reason why we love, know our commitment, not only to your love once but also to God who love us first. Because being happy and in love is not about having money but it is about having people around you who loves you and appreciate you. Love is a two way road and it needs to be reciprocated. And in life love and forgiveness always wins.

—MA. CARINA DIZON

January 12, 2021

Pulung Bulu, Angeles City

INTRODUCTION

Many writers use their poetry as a means of sharing knowledge of what they know and how they feel. At some point they use their writings to express their frustrations with the contradiction of human behavior and the bad things they experience in life. Because of the bad or the dark side of life they learn and they have shared their thoughts and views how dark side of life feels like, even look like.

No Blames For This Pain is basically a person's feeling and point of view about life, showing and made us feel the dark side of it, to enable us to feel the pain and for us to walk with the author's footstep in undergoing such feeling of lost, regrets, troubled. Even to question once existence and life's purpose.

This book would barely raise an eyebrow, but in its period it would have been viewed as a reminder to us to constantly see the positivity of experiencing that wicked feeling, for us to realize that in life we need to see and to experience such dark side, in order for us to learn and discover what life has to offer, to see the light again.

We even forget to appreciate how good life is, but these Soul Sentiments Series are masterpiece. Despite his wicked feelings for those dark experiences, those regrets, failures even lost, still goes ahead with his life. The writer even realizes that he can never restore the past, he tried to walk away but at the end of the day he chooses to face all the hardships in life.

An author once said that *"You can't see the glory of life if you haven't seen the dark side of it"*

CONTENTS

A GENTLE ULTIMATUM

At last we have arrived

In this exact moment

Of constant peace.

In our slumber

We submerge into a

Phantasmagoria of events;

Slices of our lives

Which we now wear as

Pieces of a general reflection.

We see our sanities

Being tested

And pushed to limits

And points where we start

To question our fate.

We see our triumphs,

Even those which seem

Insignificant at first glance

But those were our formative experiences

Which hold a special place

In our means of adornment

And appreciation.

We see those

Whom we have shared

An interesting life with

As well as those

Who are responsible

For any damage we received

In our hearts

Our emotions

Along with those

Whom we have found disturbing.

Now we place ourselves

In the arms of fate.

And as we do so,

Our worries emerge

From their lurking

Coming from our subconscious

And creeps its way to our shoulders,

Maniacally mocking us

And jokes of damnation.

Rest assured

That in the glory we've weaved

In the length of our lives

We will be recognized

Regardless

For we are a species

Overflowing with an unwavering spirit

Of retaliation

And willingness to move forward.

Now,

In the arms of fate

We will be embraced

And honored for our valiancy.

For we,

Our spirits,

Never surrendered

And never will it die out.

DEAR SLEEPER

Sleep to stay away

From this world which would not.

Take notice

Of my heart and how it no longer beats.

The disappearance of its rhythm

Alarms only my ears.

Pulse long gone

For ten, twelve years.

Dead since sixteen.

News travelled slow.

A cut-out obituary page lost in transit.

How could I know?

Sleep

To stay

Awake

In this world which would.

THE PRETTIEST FLOWERS DIE THE EARLIEST

Why do the good people pass before almost everyone else?

Innocent babies, good-natured toddlers, the best

Spouses that can possibly be.

You'll be surprised at how many children say

That they'll pick the prettiest flower in the garden.

From this I sense the unfairness of life, death.

But as I notice how death comes for us all.

Just on different times and ways.

Comes a newfound appreciation for life and time,

Time is too short for those who fear.

Time is too long for those who grieve.

But for those who love and are loved, time is eternity.

The sadness of present days,

Is locked and set in time

And moving to the future.

Will definitely be a slow and painful climb.

Time will need a head start to heal.

This will be a wound that will never go entirely away.

But we can only learn to hurt a little less day by day.

Though your heart won't let the sadness slide away.

The tears dry, but the memories will always stay.

We fill our hearts with the greatest of pain.

But God hears only so few.

We cry before God to know why.

But he only knows the reason why.

The young, the old they walk side by side.

Knowing someday, we shall see them all.

Death is hard. But what can we do?

DISTANT ADMIRATION

I can only dream

Of living with your

God-given beauty

But what does it mean

To be truly beautiful?

What does it mean?

To truly appreciate beauty?

Perhaps it is not a necessity

To approach it directly

To outwardly state admiration;

Perhaps the very expression

Of exalting praise

Of one's appearance

Is something that ended up being

Obsolete.

In this time

In these miserable times

Where words are running out

Of context

To provide meaning

And manifest humanity itself

It is but a good practice

To admire from afar

Similar to how we appreciate

The beauty of flowers

And the majesty nature

Perhaps Beauty

Is meant to be left by itself

And to nurture it

And appreciate it

From our distance

STILL

She walks with confidence.

Standing high and free.

As tall as she can be.

She puts on her make-up.

Showers herself with pink stuff.

Her potion iPhone.

Her high-heeled shoes.

Her doll-like pretty face.

Her fashion sense and all that.

When she puts on her headphones.

She dances with the world.

In that beautiful song,

Her heart sings to the tune.

She's a princess in a lovely gown.

She's a model in her own catwalk.

She's a doll with a rosy cheek.

A girl with a gentle and quiet spirit.

But behind all the glitz and glamour,

Of her messy, chaotic world.

When the applauds cease and accolades gone.

She meditates in the stillness of her heart.

All that she ever wanted,

Was peace within her soul.

REMINDER

She needs to be loved deeply

And her inner beauty ought to be treasured

But never forget to remind her

That she is also beautiful on the surface

The sun rises behind her smile

And the sunset is in her eyes

To describe her

Is to write

Sweet poetry

About the beauty

Of life and survival

I imagine that every day I hold her

It feels as if

I am carrying the world and all the beauty in it.

DIVINITY IN MULTITUDES

God is evident

In this vast green multitude

For it shares the mystery

And his majesty it presents

Once seen as a whole.

There are also those

Who continuously go against

The divine will

And out of sheer arrogance

We act as if we have the power

To harness the surroundings

As if damaging it

Is similar to utmost control.

Like God, these vast plains

Of vegetation

Also holds wrath inwardly

Collecting every bit of dismay.

Humanity has undeniably vexed

And will eventually take us by storm

Through an unexpected

Merciless burst of vengeance.

Those who strive

To achieve that their very own divine personas

Are honored and dignified

Will share the fruits

Of years and years of patience.

In the end of things

True immortality

Which humanity has not yet achieved

Will ironically be vested

To whatever amount of nature is left.

Capable of regrowing

And Rebirth

Even after the fall

Of the last leaf.

MICA AND THE AFTERNOON SKY

Mica looked up, one afternoon,

At the sky above her.

She immediately gasped, "Wow!"

As she was struck

With awe and wonder.

Against the vast blue backdrop

Were wisps of yellow, pink, and white.

The clouds were like cotton candy.

It was such a wonderful sight!

So Mica took a picture

Of the beautiful sky up above.

And she said to herself,

"Now I can show this

To all the people I love."

37

"Now I can show this

To all the people I love."

DO YOU HEAR HER CRY?

It took me a long while.

To better the way you live.

Since you have turned hostile,

I've got no more to give.

My land is filled with waste.

My children are displaced.

They live in utter fear,

Watching friends disappear.

You treat me like a joke:

Choke me up with your smoke,

Strip me of any clothes,

And leave me with my foes.

I have become man-made,

Who serves you like a maid.

Unnatural and impure,

A disease with no cure.

Do you know how I feel?

See the scars I conceal?

I lost my rights and voice.

You leave me with no choice.

I am shaped based on greed.

In pain, I sob and bleed.

I have been infected,

Abused and neglected.

Do you hear me crying?

I am sick and dying.

You are my therapy.

Love me and set me free.

My children, I love you.

I hope you love me too.

Your mother needs you now.

Help me I'll show you how.

Recycle and conserve,

Heed the rights I deserve.

Hear my weakening voice,

Help me regain my poise.

It seems that what you do

Has more effect on you.

I am Mother Nature,

Not a human for sure.

You live the life you drain:

You breathe the air you stain,

Drink the water you soil,

And eat the food you spoil.

My gifts you must protect:

From air to ocean shelf.

My love you should respect.

Save me to save yourself.

WOES TO THE ABYSS

We venture this world

Knowing all too well

That eventually

Everything we do

Everything we will do

Will be for naught.

We throw ourselves in this

Frantic race

Over who gets to be the one

To best achieve

And satisfy

His need for a sense of purpose.

This is an intimidating race.

This is also a race

That insults our tenacity.

We roam over these vast material dimensions

Seeking purpose

And happiness

In order to achieve

Something we can be proud of

In our planned graves

Filled with glitters

And glamour.

We often tend to forget

That we are damned

To never bring these

Hints of glamour

Once our journey ends.

Every single one of us

Will be at the mercy

Of the ultimate judge

Exposing us to malice

Seeping out any forms of regret

That we might have

And ironically

We end up regretting

The opposite of who we chose to become

In our waking life.

Time is brutal.

But above all,

It is constructive.

TROUBLED

My mind's so obscure.

Time runs out and I'm not yet done...

The loud blast of music dominates the air

I'm fainting...

Pressured...

Wish I could get out of here,

Wish this moment will pass by me now.

And be gone.

Gone forever.

CLOCKWORK

When the moon light up the sky

And the sea becomes purple and bright

When the birds sing with delight

And the stars fall through your eyes

It's all so perfect

When you sleep at night

Or frustrated with life

Or having great success

Or thinking about someone

It's all so perfect

When you are heartbroken

Or sad and depressed

When you can't help but cry

Or need to be with someone

It's all so perfect

Universal clockwork

Is keeping track of your time

And with every moment of pain

Like a seed, they shall grow in time

Into something beautiful and kind

Something loving and full of joy

In time...

It's all so perfectly realized

Love all the times

That you feel something from life

For they will build perfectly

Into a story of a lifetime

That ends

In love

Everything is playing out perfectly.

THIS WRETCHED, LONELY PATH

Damnation

From contentment

Is the misery

Bore by those

Who failed to meet their expectations

Over certain circumstances.

We are badgered by our

Insecurities

Convincing ourselves

That we are bereft

Of strength

And we lack control

Over the things we need to protect

Things we need to work hard for

Things we need to achieve and suffice.

This sensation

Paralyzes us

And provides us no motivation whatsoever

To rise up from our beddings

Allowing ourselves to drown

Over our thoughts.

We labor through this

Heart-stopping pressure

As we suffocate

From how tightly it grasps

Our sanities

Disappointment dominates

Over our consciousness

And mockingly,

It tells us,

"You are overflowing with deficiencies."

Perhaps we need to embrace it

Instead of laboring through it.

Perhaps it is a means

Of making sure

We get to stay stable

And at the same time

Lifeless

Undisturbed

And calm

As we slowly drift across these perilous waters

We will remain

Like driftwood

And allow ourselves

To flow

Until we reach stable ground.

And after that

Comes our rebirth.

After that,

Comes the greatest change.

After that,

We emerge stronger

And ready.

REGRETS

Twenty-nine years

Swiftly it comes and swiftly it goes

Your youth passed by so quickly

Like only a touch of a thousand years

You fought the battle fair and brave

Yet you weren't able to stand infirmity to the very end

The affliction seems a cross you need to bear

It destroys the core of your being confidence, hope

and reason for living

My soul fills with regrets

To watch a friend struggle in distress

Find your peace beautiful soul!

'Til one day soon in paradise we meet

IF ONLY

I don't understand why it is so difficult now.

When before it might not have been easy.

But it by far was never this bad.

I can't hear the whisper anymore.

I don't know if I ever will again.

Why can't I wake myself up?

I haven't cried in a long time.

I haven't truly expressed any type of emotion.

Except for anger.

In a long time.

I don't remember myself anymore.

I miss a lot of things.

If I knew back then.

What I was going to be like now.

I would run like hell.

And try to change a lot of things.

I regret the day the world fell upon my shoulders.

There are so many regrets.

Far more than just this short list.

I'm in a moment of life

Where things never seem to get any better.

There are still the same unsolved problems as yesterday.

And life still doesn't get any easier.

The best I can do for now,

Is smile,

And pretend like nothing really matters.

CANVAS

We began with such an empty canvas

Filled eventually with

Our cries and wails

Over affection.

We eventually learned

How to walk a straight path

Taking our sweet time

To get ourselves

From one destination

To another.

However,

As we take

This seemingly innocent path

We notice how it bares

Its fangs on us

Proving itself merciless

And cruel.

We stumble over these

Shards of broken dreams

We failed to fulfill

Bleeding as we push forward

Engaging this harsh

Cruel trek.

Our cries and wails

Now reaches its prime

Introducing us to a more

Genuine form of sadness –

Melancholy –

As we continuously labor through

These blockades.

Our canvas

Ended up getting soiled

By accidents

By our poor strokes

Done out of our

Lack of dexterity.

But maybe the chaos

Is something that connects

Every piece of our lives with each other

Maybe through these labors

Can we fully own

Our canvases

With full pride over it.

Until then

We will keep on letting our brushes

Run its own course

For we are the artists

And at the same time

The curators

Of our own

Unique experiences.

Ergo,

Life

Is something we fully own

And control.

THE DAWN

The wind blows,

And feels like ice.

And the people are still fast asleep,

Half dreaming.

If you get to see it outside,

There is nothing but total darkness.

I wonder why men awake first,

Than women do.

In this place where men dominate

The most.

Why do I see men alone?

All men and "old men" to be exact.

Some went to take a shower.

Some went to see the serenity of

The outside sea.

Get to relax, reflect and reconcile

With nature.

While some enjoy a cup of coffee

And cigarette at the table.

Its 3am.

Almost 4 in my watch.

This nautical boy I saw.

Passing around from one bed to another.

Searching for like something but nothing.

And again, I hear this noisy sound of

The machine.

That seems like with no ending....

Still... 4 hours to go, 4 hours to wait.

I can now see the dawn.

The beginning of a new day.

And we'll finally be home... home at last.

This is gonna be life.

Things...

People...

Circumstances...

They just come and go.

And happens the way the creator writes it in

The palm of his Mighty hands.

And what more can I say?

Live this life.

Make it count.

'Coz nothing else will do.

And nothing else will matter.

LIFE, PURPOSE, COMMITMENT.

Tell me about the traffic.

Tell me about your boss.

Tell me about the job.

You've wanted to quit for how many years.

Tell me.

Tell me how blessed are we to have tragedy.

So small it can fit on the tips of our tongues.

When you feel like your guardian.

Angel put in his two weeks notice two months ago.

And just decided not to tell you,

Remember,

You will survive,

Things could be worse,

And we are never given

Anything we can't handle.

Remember,

You are still here.

You are still alive.

So act like it.

PASSION INCARNATE

We are a race

That personifies character

And value

Through our actions

We are capable of shaping

What it means to be dedicated

Through our sheer persistence

And discipline over our craft

We become the incarnates

Of the very values

We swore to immortalize

Through our personalities

We can shape out

What it means

To have emotion

In essence

Our faces are unpredictable

Very difficult to read

The only chance we have

To get a read on our intentions

Is seeing the reflection

The varying curves of the face

The number of wrinkles

The enlargement and shrinking of the nostrils

The sharpening of the gaze

Through man's portal

To his soul

- The eyes

This will provide us

With their pure emotions

Combining both persona

And practice

Will give rise

To a whole new different incarnate

Someone who has the will

To allow himself to be damaged

And to be vulnerable

Using only the moral reserves

Sustained by sheer passion

This incarnate

Will deny al discouragement

Even challenging the boundaries

Of reality itself

Looking at it straight in the eye

And calmly asking it

To move out in his way

This incarnate is not blind

In fact

This incarnate

Has the clearest vision

That permeates through the present

And pierces through

Towards his preferred future

This incarnate

Is someone blessed

With an insatiable hunger

To strive for more

And to do better

72

EDUCATOR'S SONG

A season of isolation

I sit down and contemplate

Trying to reminisce...

Rooms are deserted

Hallways are empty

The silence deafening

I hear my heart sobbing...

This craft that I love so much

Will there be brighter days ahead for us?

To see my offspring, my beloved

Will everything be back

To how it was?

THE BEAUTY OF SWEET LABOR

The beauty of sweet labor,

Is the beauty of a minor.

Dream turned quietly.

Aside at the end of the day,

The beauty of the small,

Impossible ledgers recording.

Hope against subtraction and finally

Closed with a sigh.

Every unremarkable donut shop

Is somebody's act of faith,

And somewhere between almost and

Never quite, in the last miles

Of aging neon and plastic.

Backlit signage, here

Too is poetry, where the books

Will someday be balanced and the future.

Is always a bargain, everything.

Ninety-nine cents.

Look them over, the wise and great,

They take their food from a common plate

And similar knives and forks they use,

With similar laces they tie their shoes,

The world considers them brave and smart.

But you've all they had when they made their start.

You can triumph and come to skill,

You can be great if only you will,

You're well equipped for what fight you choose,

You have legs and arms and a brain to use,

And the man who has risen, great deeds to do

Began his life with no more than you.

You are the handicap you must face,

You are the one who must choose your place,

You must say where you want to go.

How much you will study the truth to know,

God has equipped you for life, But He

Lets you decide what you want to be.

Courage must come from the soul within,

The man must furnish the will to win,

So figure it out for yourself, my lad,

You were born with all that the great have had,

With your equipment they all began.

Get hold of yourself, and say: "I can."

ODE TO YOUNG AGE

Marvel at the glory of age

Rendering all it dominates over

To remember

And to learn from their past.

Perhaps the best memory

Most people often enjoy

Is their time of youth

As well as their formative years.

We relish over how simple it was

Being children

Unaware of the ills of society

And the inevitable human nature.

Perhaps the reason why it is the period of time

We are most fond of

Is the purity in which childhood holds

At some point in our lives

We were bereft of any separating marks

That compels most people

To hate and discriminate against.

At some point in our lives

We were at our prime in terms of

Being true to what we say

Bearing no malice or ill contempt

We thrive on the purity of trust

And the truest form of truth.

Perhaps these memories

Are expressions

Of what used to be possible

And what is still possible even now.

Given that all of us are damned

In such a cruel, merciless world

We rely on the memories of childhood

For recleansing.

And to rekindle purity,

Above all.

Perhaps that is what it means

To be a child.

NOSTALGIA

I was stunned when I saw him.

He looks not exactly the same the last

Time my memory remembers of him.

He awakens the child in me again.

Pure and innocent.

And all the memories of young life

Keep flashing through my mind.

Forever beautiful...eternal.

GROWTH

I can not pinpoint the moment when

I stopped being a kid.

Maybe it was high school,

When I started,

Wide eyed and naive,

Scared and alone and knowing fully well that

None of my friends liked me.

Sitting at lunch with these girls.

I was desperate to please

But not quite fitting in.

Maybe it was middle school

When I suddenly realized that

Life is hard

And my life, like the

Whirlwind it seemed to be

Left me stranded.

Struggling to keep up with coursework

Struggling to keep up with friends

Struggling to remember that I

Was just as smart

And worthy as these other kids.

Or maybe it was fourth grade

When my anxiety disorder came into play

When I was so afraid to fail my tests I started

Pulling out my hair and I haven't stopped since.

I did not grow up because I wanted to

But I was so afraid to fail

That I had to.

I did grow up because I wanted to

And if I could go back to

Being clueless in my

Childhood naivety

I would do it in a heartbeat

But I can't.

And I can not pinpoint the moment when

I stopped being a kid

And as terrifying as it is,

Maybe I still have more.

Growing up left to do.

COMRADES AND JUDASES

We began this life

Surrounded by enigmas.

It is only logical

For us to live our whole lives

Continuously meeting

Random people

And be mystified

And terrified

Of their great and obvious differences.

We tend to grow based on the pace

Of our pack.

However, there will come a time

Where your bonds

Will be tested

By the chaos that will eventually

Consume all of you.

In this respect

Everyone

Including those whom you shared

A great amount of peril with

Will soon turn out to be

People wearing masks

And removing them at the sight of comfort.

In this epiphany

We grew offended

And hurt

For all this time

That you were surrounded

By those who claimed that they were with you

Were only there because

You were a necessity.

You were a necessity

So essential

That it is easy for you to be commodified

And used.

Those who betray

Find joy in the success

And fulfillment

Of their insidious agenda

Against you.

Snakes.

Luckily, you also found people

Who remained by your side

Out of pure intent.

The irony is that

These people

Emerged from the same

Traumatic womb of experiences

Your betrayers have emerged from initially.

This must be the reason why

We are filled with both

Friends and foe

For their current identities

The current choices they make

Were made out of the results

Of emerging from that chaos

And how it changed them.

Therefore the chaos in life

Is the one who gives birth

To both.

So it is downright absurd

For us to choose

Who will remain by our side

And who will stab our backs.

Because time itself is a harsh judge

And all of them

Including yourself

Are at the mercy of time's

Damaging offensives.

NOT MEANT TO STAY

We are no longer

On the same wavelength.

In fact, I don't think we ever were.

You are like an old boutique I saw once,

And happened to pass by again.

I bought a few trinkets as I did before,

And you also got what you were aiming for.

And a shop will close as almost all shops do.

It's time for me to get going too.

BECAUSE WHY NOT?

A best friend is always there,

Whether you need advice, or a pep talk,

Or even a shoulder to cry on.

A best friend listens with her heart

And is always honest with you,

Even though the truth may not be

What you want to hear.

A best friend knows all your secrets,

Understands your fears share your dreams.

A best friend never stops believing in you

Even if you give up on yourself.

You are that kind of friend to me.

And no matter what happens, you always will be.

You are my best friend....

My forever friend.

Because you are my friend,

My life is enriched in a myriad of ways.

Like a cool breeze on a sweltering day,

Like a ray of sunshine parting glowering clouds,

You lift me up.

In good times, we soar,

Like weightless balloons

Over neon rainbows.

In bad times, you are soothing balm

For my pummeled soul.

I learn so much from you;

You help me see old things in new ways.

I wonder if you are aware

Of the bright seeds you are sowing in me.

I'm a better person for knowing you,

So that everyone I interact with

Is touched by your good effect on me.

You relax me, refresh me, and renew me.

Your bounteous heart envelops me

In joy, love and peace.

May your life be filled

With dazzling blessings,

Just as I am blessed

By being your friend.

I'll be by your side

Because why not?

UNASSAILING LOVE

Oh what joy it would be

To be loved without any need

To recompensate.

It is tiring

To live in a world

That continuously

Consumes you

In your entirety.

As we succumb

To the dread of loneliness

And solitude

We find solace

In the arms

Of pure

Unadulterated love

That admires us for the essence

Of being ourselves.

They are those

Who are the incarnates of

What we have to be for ourselves;

Regardless of the merit

Regardless of the gift

Regardless of anything bestowed.

Still

This burning desire

To love

And be loved

Holds no definition upon it.

And in itself

It is already worth the marvel.

IN ANOTHER LIFE

In another life,

Maybe you and I exist.

In another life,

Maybe we will see each other.

In another life,

Maybe I can hug you for real.

In another life,

Maybe you and I are meant to be.

In another life,

Maybe I can hold your hand, kiss you tenderly,

And hear your heart beating,

Telling me I'm no longer dreamin'

In another life...

Maybe...

Maybe...

BOOK

She's a poetry book.

You must read every letter

And digest every word.

Every beautiful part of her paints a part of a bigger picture.

You can't love her if you don't intend on reading every page.

And learning how to comprehend every piece of her.

There are few things in this world

As adventurous

As exploring her mind.

THE JOY OF BEING HAPPY

What does it mean

To truly form a smile?

Does it involve romance

Or perhaps a hint of pride?

How can we tell

That someone

Is truly happy

By its essence?

Perhaps we can ask them

What they are grateful for happening

And how much

Do their regrets weight?

Does happiness mean

That gratitude should dominate

Over regret?

Or is regret something

That enables us to never be satisfied

And therefore we are urged

To continue on to our paths

Until we see the very end of it.

We do not realize that by doing so

We end up evolving

Into those who are blessed

With so much mortality

And death

To a point that we continuously

Set new heights for us

To conquer

And endure.

Perhaps true joy

Can only be achieved

If we get to choose

Which paths we have to take

Despite all the chaos that awaits

At least

We get to choose.

At least,

We get to set a standard

And choose over what labors

We have to go through

In order to bring ourselves

To greater heights.

CHASING NATURE

And the wind began to blow cold;

And all we see was green.

Up, up and away we go,

Far from the city life,

The stress of school

And the worries at home.

The view of the whole city

Was like a portrait of the greatest

Painter ever lived.

City lights dancing;

Like I've only seen them from my dreams.

It awed me to see

How magnificent the sun is,

Ruler of all creations!

As I witness it rises in the east,

With its rays pointing from every direction

In the sky.

How majestic!

Everything was just so perfect,

A salute to The One who made it!

WHAT IS HAPPINESS?

Happiness is a smile plastered across your face.

Happiness in you is seeing happiness in others.

Happiness is accepting who you are.

Happiness is love.

Happiness is being content with what you have.

Happiness is knowing that no matter what,

Someone is there to hold you tightly.

Happiness is money.

Happiness is your house.

Happiness is your car.

Happiness is the parties you throw.

Happiness is solitude.

Happiness is not poisoning yourself

With everything in the world around you.

Happiness begins with sacrificing my whole life,

Happiness begins with bidding loneliness goodbye;

Happiness begins with crying all my tears away,

My true happiness only begins with you everyday...

It's no question true happiness may not sound real,

Something very hard to wait for and keep still,

But you are the one, who gave me something to feel,

True happiness began with you as the Lord revealed.

Happiness begins with declaring your arms my home,

Happiness begins with no need in being all alone,

Happiness begins with companion, who believes in us,

My true happiness only begins with earning your trust.

ASTRAL PLAINS

We are vessels

Blessed with two souls:

One with the power

To be shaped

And grow

And age;

One with the power

To defy time

And mold the very fabric of it

Through sheer will alone.

We live in this material world

Through this material vessel

Stimulated by its pleasure

Destroyed by its ills

Shaking our moralities

To the bone.

And at the same time

We do not live in this reality.

In fact

Through simply denying it

And hoping for growth

Hoping for something better

Hoping to grasp something so greedily

Is what lies

In our subconscious.

In this state

We become unrivaled

And everything we say and do

Becomes true to the last word

Everything we admire

We are able to become

And in this respect

Selfishness, greed

Is non-existent.

In this state

It can become a form of love

To the self

Being so passionate about this

Self-love

To a point that

We embrace the sin of greed.

The major predicament

Of those who frequent these astral plains

Is lacking the ability

To shape these ideals into reality.

There are some who fell before the abyss

Of idealism

Not being able to stand

At the balance

Of both reality

And fantasy.

And there are those

Who became madly immersed

In reality

Being veterans of the tight rope

That thin line

Between rationality

And blind ambition.

These are gods

Who are able to will their dreams

Into existence

Through the use of their sheer will alone.

These are the true masters

Of both life

And the astral plains.

A NIGHT'S HAPPY SONG

I love the skies tonight;

The clouds are like cotton balls up above,

Stars twinkle near and far

And the moon's so big

And shining so bright.

I think of the creator,

As I sit under the cold breeze of the night.

After a few minutes...

The clouds transformed.

Like a spilled flour!

Oh, how I love God's creations!

Wish there was ever a shooting star;

And I'd be lost into a world of imaginations...

HISTORY, TOMORROW, AND FOREVER

A maiden sat in the sunset glow

Of the shadowy, beautiful Long Ago,

That we see through a mist of tears.

She sat and dreamed, with lips apart,

With thoughtful eyes and a beating heart,

Of the mystical future years;

And brighter far than the sunset skies

Was the vision seen by the maiden's eyes?

There were castles built of the summer air,

And beautiful voices were singing there,

In a soft and floating strain.

There were skies of azure and fields of green,

With never a cloud to come between,

And never a thought of pain;

There was the music, sweet as the silvery notes

That flows from a score of thrushes' throats.

But the castles built of the summer wind

I have vainly sought. I only find

Shadows, all grim and cold; –

For I was the maiden who thought to see

Into the future years, – Ah, me!

And I am grey and old.

My dream of earth was as fair and bright

As my hope of heaven is to-night.

The hands that I thought to clasp are crossed,

The lips and the beautiful eyes are lost,

And I seek them all in vain.

The gushes of melody, sweet and clear,

And the floating voices, I do not hear,

But only a sob of pain;

And the beating hearts have paused to rest.

Yet dreams are but dreams at the very best.

LUCKY

A part of me has always been fulfilled,

This work helped me keep up to what I built,

I am able to break down the walls that were made of concrete bricks,

And dared to emerge every time I feel like I am about to shrink.

For me, this is more than just a job.

For me, it blossoms the passion I already have.

It paves the way and helps me see my own dream path.

And through this, I found a reason to be happy and laugh.

I knew there are so many people wondering where to go.

I didn't have clarity on what they should do.

Somehow life teaches you something until you know.

So you have the courage to face challenges that seemed bizarre and new.

To have this work has always been a pleasure.

It leads me towards victory, and prospects always drew closer.

I managed to push problems in a place that's further.

I knew this represents my further endeavor.

I see myself taking every day as a chance to work hard—

For I acknowledge that in every good deed, there's always a reward.

Life will trail me to the best position I could not disregard.

And I will enjoy life along with my sincere heart.

I know every moment I get to spend on my work,

Bravery and profound knowledge will always lurk.

I will pair my courage with willingness and effort.

And see where it'll take me in this vast world.

ONCE UPON AN INNOCENCE

Sun shines brightly in the horizon

Wind touches my face as I sniffed this fragrance

It was not long since I went to this pond

The remembrance lives in me as I recall all the memories

The ground where I used to step my shoes filled with mud

Face covered with grease from the gates and fences

Running like a cheetah in this endless time

If only I could be little, I'll do this all over again

Those people who used to yell my name

I wish I can hear them again

But those moments were long gone

I now have a child ready to face challenges from the outside

Green grasses welcome every child

Leaves falling beneath the heart of an innocent

As I watch him running with his arms wide open

Surely I used to be like him, now it's his time to make new memories

BACK TO INNOCENT DAY

Our childhood memories hold so much innocence.

They hold the best laughter; we didn't have fears.

It was just pure bliss; we get along to the world as it spins.

As we embraced moments as it was, didn't care who'll lose or win.

We sometimes miss the days we were still kids.

The times we were carefree like birds testing their wings.

We could stay all day on our favorite playground- enjoy that rusty swings,

As we listen to how the wind sings.

Our happiness was not luxurious since then.

We didn't care to commit the same mistakes again.

Every chance we get —we felt so overwhelmed.

We didn't care much about the realm.

Those were the golden days —our irreplaceable youth.

These days when we still manage to move on from the hurtful truth,

Back to the days when we're able to emerge through.

They hold our proof of how much we grew.

Those pigtail days are now gone.

For it feels like we're all up for a run.

All this adulthood that can't be undone.

We have happiness, and now we have none.

All these scars that remained on our knees

Tell a story —such profound memories.

These childhood memories are enough to put our hearts at ease—

For we are up to reality to live up to our dreams.

INFINITE CONNECTION

Our distance did not matter

You became so close to my heart for as long as I can remember

Lucky I am to have you as my partner both in sunny and rainy days

You will be there whatever the case

Time may say that each is becoming rusty

That's not true cause ours seem to survive despite of modernity

What I love is that we were like fairies

Being there for each other when the other one is weary

No one can ever replace you, my pal

Every moment doesn't seem so dull

My stomach aches as I laugh so hard to our nonsense jokes

Every moment is treasured every time we spoke

We may have different paths and horizons to uncover

But you will always be my sister

I cannot wait to meet you there at the top

Having our proudest moment because we did a good job

SAVED BY UNDYING LOVE

My world was once filled with darkness and silence

Until you came around with a torch in your hand

I was alone and no one to turn to but the edge of this invisible presence

A woman who was shipwrecked and unconsciously lying in the sand

Each day, my hope would slowly fade away

But it seems that you just lighted up my way

You gave me a new life to look forward to

Always grateful to share and cherish moments with you

It is when our skins touched when I feel the flames ignite

It is when you kiss my lips, my pulse rise

How wonderful is tonight

I'll be forever yours until our demise

A promise not to let you go

The moment our eyes met I knew that you are not a foe

Foolish it may be to someone tainting what we have

But here I am, endlessly offering you my purest love

THROUGH IT ALL

When you love someone, all poems will suddenly rhyme,

All horizons will meet on the same line,

And your heart will beat in such ways that you can't define.

But always put God in the center, and everything will be fine.

When you love someone, everything will fall right in place,

You will have someone who will love you on your worst phase,

You will wake up next with the love you have and see such a wonderful face,

God will always stay by your side and will run with you at any race.

When you love someone, love will give you the rightest poetry,

Someone you could call on, may it be on night and day.

Someone you know who will be there with you and will stay,

Always empower your love through prayers every day.

When you love someone, all your scars will heal from the past,

All ugly memories will vanish like clouds of dust,

God will always give you guidance and a clear mind,

To always stand guard and bless you with a heart that is kind.

When you love someone, you'll forget about your pain,

On days when you became the only person left to blame.

You will have a home you could run to when it rains.

All things happen for a reason, just understand every challenge that came.

When you love someone, you know it's something that'll last forever,

Someone that you know God fated to meet together.

Always remember there's no perfect love, but it's now or never.

Just stay strong and take each other as an inspiration to be better.

WANDERING THE SCENE OF ELATION

Feeling like the whole world is mine

My feet are up on the ground

The beats that I hear from the streets have my body moving non-stop

There's no pain, just joy from around

This is just a dream come true

Greeting everybody with a smile

That's what I do

Sharing the happiness I could to inspire me and you

Feels so good to be alive in this merry land

No room for anything that makes a person blue

Some people find blissful moments in a single thought

Children singing their hearts out

Busy traffic lights that seems to follow a melody

How lucky I am to live in this place filled with music

Such wonderful beings I see, blossoming friendships I sense

I just hope I could stay in this forever

Feeling the warmth of welcome from each individual

Wrapping their arms to one another as they walk towards their destination

Happiness is when you feel you are loved

It is when you appreciate little things constantly

ATTAINABLE HAPPINESS

Staying under the sun's heat.

Relishing all promises kept.

Writing plans on an empty sheet.

My happiness always comes cheap.

Books I could endlessly read.

Lessons from scars that still bleed.

Sights of rivers that's too deep.

My happiness always comes so cheap.

Paintings on museums that take the lead.

Sun is rising every morning in the east.

Memories that keep replaying inside my head.

My happiness always comes so cheap.

A long good night's sleep.

A nice food as my self-treat.

Words that is sincere and sweet.

My happiness always comes so cheap.

A good cup of coffee is all I want to get.

Unrushed walk on a lobby with calmness on the blend.

A worthwhile movie that won't lullaby me to sleep

My happiness always comes so cheap.

A right playlist I can't skip.

A stirred-well green tea I could sip.

A life I don't desire to quit.

My happiness always comes so cheap.

GLIMPSE OF ASPIRATIONS

Slowly I grabbed the shield which I held for years

It is a fight for a yes or no

Been shedding a lot of tears

Thinking if I should stop or go

Chasing all the butterflies is not that easy

Countless obstacles will make you feel more than queasy

Monsters will bring you down non-stop

But you gotta fight your way to the top

Deepest waters you are about to swim

Thousands mountains you will climb

Somewhat unbelievable like an action film

Yet you have to understand that fulfilling goals is not a crime

From this day on, I promise not to give up

Walls I will break and no one can interrupt

Inspired by people who truly cared

I will make sure that my name would be heard

LOOKING FORWARD TO

I am a person whose heart is filled with dreams.

And enthusiasm has its own screams.

I always knew I could understand the in-betweens.

And look forward to the future that I am capable to achieve.

When I was a kid, I used to dream of shallow things.

To be part of something that my skill perfectly fits.

To be in a competition where I see never-ending wins.

And move forward through all of these years.

When I slowly grew up, my dreams changed.

Suddenly, all these hollow things I need to rearrange.

I need to savor life's challenges, and it's after taste.

And unhinged tomorrow is something I need to face.

I want to have my own home someday in a faraway place,

Where it'll be filled with many trees that would give me the best shade.

The thought of it was enough for my present struggle to fade.

And someday soon, my success will be known so as my name.

I will keep my passion flaring as my fire still burns.

I will show the world the things I am capable to serve.

I will show them I could be better —never worse.

And that I am good at everything —I don't care if it will hurt.

I will live my life in my own terms.

Someday soon, I know it'll be my turn.

For now, I have to hold on to my strength and remain firm.

For life is teaching me something that I need to learn.

TIME TICKS

Time ticks, seconds turn into a minute.

Have you ever gone to that place you always want to visit?

Or you're just taking these doors that refer to many exits?

And didn't dare to dismantle all these limits.

Time ticks, minutes turn into an hour.

Have you ever said the words you want to say louder?

Have you said all these confessions sealed in a letter?

Or you're just slowly running away so you won't remember?

Time ticks, hours turn into a day.

Have you ever wondered about the chances and possible ways?

Have you thought about adventures and why you should not stay?

Or you're just too worried to risk, so you sulk in your greys?

Time ticks, days turn a week.

Have you ever tried to condition your tired feet?

Have you ever tried walking away from your troubles at a faster speed?

Or you just sat there, silently calling yourself weak?

Time ticks, weeks turn into months.

Have you ever muddled over the things you truly want?

Have you listened to how your mind and heart respond?

Or you just stood there, thanking all of your wrong cards?

Time ticks, moths turn into a year.

It's been so long, but you're still stranded here.

Still unhappy, so much time wasted and callings you refused to hear.

You gave no risk and wasted so many times wishing all struggles will disappear.

HEADING TO A MEANINGFUL LIFE

We are all lost souls finding the real meaning of life.

We travel so far to reach the highest heights.

We stay up late to talk to the stars at night.

We knew that after all, we'd be facing different fights.

We spend our days looking for different signs.

We are trying to read something that's between the lines,

As well as understood the meanings behind all these rhymes.

And we search for the meaning of life at a perfect time.

We all look forward to running thousands of miles.

We all want to have our stand under our own lights.

And see optimism no matter how bright or gloomy the skies,

As we wake up every day to live and rise.

Some days are imperfect, and some nights are sad.

But we need to wake up with motivation and just be glad.

We have to understand the past that we already had.

And move forward despite how the world sometimes sounded so mad.

You might deal with things that would make you unhappy.

But you'll get by because life's not just tragedy.

We all learn from the wrong decisions that we create from yesterday.

Perhaps, that's how we should face reality.

Our purpose in life changes often.

It will make you hard at times, or it helps you soften.

And we will all find all the reasons for living because we're chosen.

And enjoy the best of everything as we take all the lessons

PRODUCTIVE LIVING

I hear the birds chirping from above, a new day it is

Tires screeching, horns honking

Streets are noisy as you fix your tux

Shiny as your shoes are, as you step out at the side road

Waiting for a single automobile to pass by

"Good day!' you say

Wearing a smile on that visage

Papers laying on your desk waiting for your signs

You smiled beneath the tension running through your veins

Took a deep breath, you are indeed primed

Started a conversation with your computer

You answered through tapping your keyboard

Suddenly you let out a sigh, seems you need a little break

Stared beyond the glass window

Towering vehicles and people who are shouting their lungs out

Y'all tired but empowered by goals that yet to be fulfilled

To work hard every day

To turn sunrise into sundown

Erasing "rest" to your vocabs

Loving the idea of being worn out for it is already imprinted in your very soul

AUTHOR OF EXISTENCE

Sitting on my favorite chair

Got my pen and journal ready to write anew

It would be a long day before I went back to my lair

Everybody pictures me as someone who always care

Sometimes I tend to forget myself

Thinking about everything that comes in my way

Truly I have written so many diaries which can be

place in a single shelf

Staring at the ceiling had no clue what to say

I live for everyone, pleasing them everyday

Drastic as it may be

My attitude and personality

But wherever I turn around there are rules of reality to obey

For every living soul that fights for survival

Needs to bring confidence for his journey

To figure out things that seems and sees

That you have to be yourself in any trial

I know I am not alone in this battle

I just have to know myself better

Weigh my actions so in the end there would be no

room for the word, "startle"

Go and appreciate yourself, lad and make yourself a thank you letter

CHAIN LOVE

Of broken wings,

And broken dreams,

Of misconceptions of life

And reality

Such things were interchanged

Such feelings were played.

Do tears have to shed?

Do hearts need to be shattered?

Is happiness something to chase for?

Life's not always a bed of roses.

And love's not always joy and pure bliss.

UNTAMED PAIN

Is there any way to make the pain stop?

I keep going down; I thought I was supposed to go up.

All these roads I've been through were just too rough.

It made me want to collapse instead of becoming tough.

For now, I lost all reasons to smile.

I stopped waiting for my positivity to shine.

I knew nobody cares if I'm alive or fine,

I grew so tired of my pain but all I did was hide.

Nobody asked if I was okay.

It's like I was nobody's listening to what I pray.

All these people gave me a reason to feel betrayed.

They all walked away after, yet their damages stayed.

All I could remember were the days I grew so weak.

All these storms that never turned bleak.

Somehow I stopped waiting for days to turn into a week,

Same old stories, to them I am still a wreck.

I am an abandoned home they tend to burn.

Since all of my errors and failures keep on taking turns.

Even I stopped listening to what I yearn.

All I feel is a tired body, the hearts too worn.

I keep suffering from the idea that I wasn't worthy of love,

And I am nothing regardless of what I already have.

For them, I was just made of another sterner stuff.

They keep leaving me because they think I wasn't enough.

AFRAID

Most of us have always been too afraid.

That someone will be there to rain our on parade.

Too scared to see how we will love when they played.

Too afraid to get drown in the puddles they made,

We are afraid that of what the world will say.

It's like they planted fences on all of our ways.

We're too worried about how they'll ruin our days.

So we allowed them to trap us in their maze.

It's ironic how we are too frightened of judgment.

When honestly, they didn't know where were truly went.

They don't know the story behind the hours we spent.

They didn't know how we tried hard until we bent.

Perhaps, people are there to show their dismay.

They're like a ticking grenade.

Anytime soon, everything around will be slain.

Just like us, insecurities and intimidation are they are made.

So we keep living being watched by microscopic eyes,

But despite the threat of judgment, I hope we manage to arise.

We need to listen to what our hearts want and despise.

So we get encouraged to turn into strengths our entire silent sighs.

If we allow judgment to stop us from reaching the highs.

We will never learn —we will never turn wise.

We will emerge from all the nights that were enveloped by loud cries.

And make them our inspiration why we should try.

WHAT HAPPENS

I used to think about what happens if we die.

Will we get all the answers to our "why?"

Will I finally see a better color of the sky?

And to the pain, can I just run away or just fly?

I used to think about what happens if we die.

Will I get that chance to say goodbye?

Will I give people a reason to cry?

Will I able to hear all the truths from their lies?

I used to think about what happens if we die.

Is heaven really that high?

Are there still rains during July?

Do all flowers there wither and turn dry?

I used to think about what happens if we die.

Will I get to meet someone I could rely?

Will I be able to get by?

Will sadness and loneliness I can defy?

I used to think about what happens if we die.

Will I get the chance to say the words I try to deny?

Will I understand the lessons it tried to imply?

Will I manage to get my desired reply?

I used to think about what happens if we die.

Will we be able to meet good guys?

Is happiness up there is something we could buy?

Will we be able to find acceptance nearby?

MY HEART

My heart is the scariest part of me.

It holds so much depth just like the sea.

I don't know which sight it prefers to see.

Sometimes, it doesn't feel free.

My heart could hold so much anger.

Sometimes, the reasons reassemble danger.

It painted my nights with the faces of a stranger.

It's like a dark place —a ghostly chamber.

My heart never forgets.

All these faces, voices, and sounds of regrets.

It never forgets how it made me upset.

It never forgets all the heartaches it gets.

My heart sometimes forgets how to forgive.

It keeps wondering how I lost everything when I start to give.

It never ceases to remember how all of them leave.

It never forgives those who gave me heartaches to grieve.

My heart gets to carry so much madness.

It reaches to the point that I neglected my happiness.

It never forgets how they made me feel so less.

And how they highlighted that I was nothing but a mess.

My heart suddenly felt so lonely and empty.

Although the thoughts in my head were too hefty.

I didn't know why my heart carries anger way too plenty.

This anger made me cruel as well —it made me

hopelessly petty.

NO BLAMES FOR THIS PAIN

I don't want to blame you for this pain.

We all make choices, sometimes we don't need to explain.

You left and yes, it leaves me a constant rain.

When I realize it's not me whom you choose —not once again.

I don't want to blame you why my heartaches.

Maybe I can't force love to stay when it's meant to break.

It just happens that your perspective changed its pace,

It's not truly your fault why your heart ran out of space.

I don't want to blame you for leaving first.

Maybe you silently battled all of your monsters and worse.

It's just that you ran out of strength to disburse.

And it was never really your fault why I am hurt.

I don't want to blame you for my vacancy.

Maybe I just need to deal with the truths that I see.

It's not your fault why I'm still awake in the morning at three.

Maybe love is not always fair —not always guaranteed.

I don't want to blame you for these screams.

I can't hate you for giving me no reasons to dance

on the sun's beams.

Perhaps, we're no longer a team.

I was never a part of your reality, not even your

dreams.

I don't want to blame you for following your heart.

It's not your fault that our love lost its art.

Perhaps, you stopped counting me as your other

half.

And not every ending gets a second start.

POISON

World of loathe,

Sympathy faded.

Restricted growth.

A heart filled with hatred.

Endless questions.

Comparison created.

Unknown intentions.

Truth fabricated.

Insecurities blossomed.

Heart grew hard.

A ground in autumn.

Dealt with wrong cards.

Happiness constrained.

Positivity obscured.

Impression stained.

Detestation lurked.

Unappreciative minds.

Competition always arises.

We stopped being kind.

Desperation to stay on highs.

Stereotypes everywhere.

Contentment compromised.

Stopped wanting to have a share.

Always setting eyes on the prize.

GETTING UP

I am finally seeing the good in goodbyes.

I started leaving these fear behind.

I learned to keep my focus despite all these securitizing eyes.

I need to condition myself that someone I need to play blind.

I want to give myself another shot of tries.

I am allowing my fate to take me where the wind blows.

I am going to grow through my rains made from my cries.

I am going to float to where this river flows.

I am going to start counting on my stars.

And start seeing the story behind my poems.

I am no longer concealing my ugly scars.

I will accept all of the flaws that I never have spoken.

I will embrace my unchangeable imperfections.

I memorized all of my black holes.

I learned to stay away from false promises and deceptions.

And everything that's out of my control.

I will gather my strength and bravery.

I will set aside all my unhealthy flaws.

I will never be afraid to get lost in reverie.

And I will rest if needed —I will take a pause.

I will learn to get my heads out of the clouds.

I will learn to stop waiting for someone to call.

I will learn to make my way out of the crowd,

And will never be afraid to break down all of my walls.

PERMANENTLY GONE

I still don't know to accept.

The more I think, the more I regret.

For losing you turned me into a shipwreck.

With hopeless voyage and broken decks.

It hurts to wake up knowing I'm still drowned.

Through the ocean floor of my thoughts is where I was found.

Everything around me became inaudible sounds.

Losing you left me with no direction to be around.

I still think about the future and you're no longer a part of it.

It feels so surreal to the point that I refused for reality to hit.

All I see was myself wanting to quit.

Because not having you anymore still aches, I must admit.

I still don't know to start again.

All that I feel is a sharp pain.

Thinking about the day you're gone, I was never sane,

My soul lost its optimism, I feel despairingly drained.

I wish I get the chance to spend a minute walk.

I wish I was able to hear your voice as you talk.

I hated myself for all the courage I never plucked.

Since all I heard were my sobs as I sulk.

Time was treacherous, death was a traitor.

My mind became an empty paper.

How can I move on when the world stopped giving me its favor?

It was too hopeless but I wish I could still see you later.

WHEN WE DIE

When we die, where do our souls first go?

Do we go back to the places we already know?

Do we allow our curiosity to flow?

Are we all allowed to see what was never shown?

When we die, do our souls pondered about going back?

Do we stop being harsh and bad?

Do we forget all the anger that flows in our blood?

When we became drifting souls, do our hearts still pound?

When we became souls, and to their eyes, we are totally gone,

Will we get another chance to change what was never done?

Do we still get excited about the upcoming dawn?

Does feeling no physical pain made us all feel like we won?

When we die, do our souls still want to take asleep?

Do we still desire to take a rest that's peaceful and slumber was gone deep?

Does it recharge us when we feel weak?

Do all our wounds no longer bleed?

When we die, do our souls finally found its escape?

Do we get a choice on which days we should partake?

Are we allowed to be free when we feel like we're about to break?

Does it cleanse us from head to toe including all our mistakes?

When we die, do our souls find its light as a guide?

Does it mean there's no need for us to hide?

All of our untamed personalities and all our words that sounded not right?

Does it mean we get to accept all our horrible sides?

FOR PEACE

In one corner of the world, there's an endless war.

Some families aren't sure if they could come home.

To be safe just like how their life was before.

But they're stranded to fight in places considered as a hot zone.

Soldiers were more like birds lost in their flight.

They fight despite having sleepless nights.

They all wished everything's over so stars could begin to shine bright.

They wanted to win a battle just so they could one day see the lights.

Still, their future was written in uncertainty that they can't read.

They keep walking on the unsure road, all these threatening streets.

All these pathways that require double speed.

All they ever wanted was peace, that's what their heart speaks.

Although their life is on the very verge.

They need to keep up to their duties, patriotism should surge.

Fear and doubts must never merge.

They need to keep fighting so peace will remain to emerge.

They have to face the days thinking straight.

They have to leave all of their personal frustrations and its weight.

They are hoping for a better world, that's what their hopes are made.

Despite the fact that they never have an uncertain happy fate.

They forget about their longings and pains,

They want to do their best so they won't hear any blames.

They only wanted a country that safe, serene, and clean.

They only wished peace that why to battlegrounds—they came.

AS WE GROW UP

The world revolved so fast.

Our welfare they didn't ask.

We're all facing schedules set on a rush.

All of sudden, we don't want to be on the last.

The world sounded so weird.

Our sentiments no longer heard.

We're all heading somewhere unclear.

Our troubles never seemed to disappear.

The world looked a little foul.

Our concerns sounded like growls.

We're all running on corners we're allowed.

Our pain we have to leave in the middle of a crowd.

The world sounded a little too loud.

Our little victories made us not proud.

We're all aiming for such unreachable clouds.

Our growth felt so sluggish —all stranded on the same grounds.

The world appeared a little demanding.

Our hearts lost hope in misunderstandings.

We're all wishing for the stars that are never listening.

Our aged made us feel like we're barefooted while drunk dancing.

The world filled with so much pressure.

Our minds never rest, our sleep's measured.

We're all seeking for happiness like it was a treasure.

Our aging years took us to places we're not ready to call endeavors.

FAIRNESS

To live a tranquil life, there's a need to be just.

We need to sweep off all the crimes and its remaining specks of dust.

We need to determine people hiding in disguise.

To humanity, perhaps we need to trust.

If a person commits a crime, what happens after?

Do they need to clean all the errors that scattered?

Does everyone paid for the mistakes, or they just manage to escape faster?

Some might have a free pass like their crimes didn't matter.

Crimes exist every day —everywhere.

Does everyone gets punished, everyone's treated fair?

Do we all get justice despite how scared?

Does everyone from the top position really care?

Does everyone get the punishment for their crimes?

Does everyone get the pay all of their fines?

Or is there something called hidden lines?

Does justice really prevail at all times?

Do rich and poor vary?

When it comes to justice, is there are contrary?

Do they consider fairness as necessary?

Or we will in a country where rich people turned truly scary?

I hope we get to live in a world where justice prevails.

Despite the turmoil, the boat of truth still sails.

I hope we get to evaluate all the given details.

So amity and righteousness remain.

RIGHT PERSON FELT LIKE HOME

And sometimes we wished we could take a pause.

From all the crisscrossing crowds and applause.

We crave silence behind painted walls.

While listening to our favorite songs.

I want to thank you for loving me real.

You always reassure I am at ease and acknowledge what I feel.

I found comfort watching you hold that steering wheel.

Heading somewhere were problems we no longer need to deal.

Comfort means having a bond with your dogs.

It's like forgetting for a while all of the odds.

We get the chance to set aside the sobs.

And conquer the day like it's made for us.

Being with you means I am safe.

With you, I am allowed to escape.

To adventures, I am allowed to create.

I thank the peace you gave me —I am glad you came.

Comfort means being with the right person.

Someone who knows how to make good conversations.

Even the silence, it gives you the relaxation.

Someone who eradicate all the complications.

For a while, I hope we will find more time to spend like this.

I hope we get the chance to take a rest.

This soothing comfort is truly the best.

I thank you for loving me with no less.

EVERYWHERE

Evil watching you from behind.

Evil invading your mind.

Evil stopped you from being kind.

Evil made you blind.

Evil standing next to you,

Evil pretending to be true.

Evil won't let you through.

Evil painted your sadness blue.

Evil stares at your from afar.

Evil started a war.

Evil reminded you of your scars.

Evil stopped you from being who you are.

Evil dancing in the dark.

Evil leaves ugly scratches and marks.

Evil killed all of your sparks.

Evil says all the bad remarks.

Evil killed your hope.

Evil made you broke.

Evil sounded like an unfunny joke.

Evil made your loneliness lurk.

Evil is everywhere.

Evil I here and there.

Evil could be him or her.

Be careful who to trust, dear.

THROBBING

And sometimes, I look at myself in the mirror and

see a stranger,

With nothing but imperfection that was left on my

skin to remember.

As I slowly scratch mistakes whose stings still

lingers.

I know I will never be enough— I know I'll never be

better.

Sometimes, my self-issues created a puddle to give

a reason for my drowning.

My morning suddenly filled with dying hopes and

endless crying.

I wasn't certain if my pain is visible —all I could hear was me slowly dying.

I wish someday, all anguish will stop coming.

I always put them first but I was never their second nor their third.

In my picture, they're the only clear thing while in theirs, I came out blurred.

To me, their problems mattered while I was just a voice to their crown, too inaudible to be heard.

They're my strengths, my emphasis, and my happiness but I was just promise that was too slurred.

I always bring them to my future, while to them; I was just another forgotten plan.

Never this someone they want to tag along, always

never enough, never a more than.

I put their secrets in my chest while they spilled

mine, always leaving the tip of their tongues.

I wish I was someone they remember when they're

left with nothing if their world shuns.

I wasn't sure why they have to leave a cut that runs

so deep

I was aiding their wounds while they're only

watching mine as they bleed.

I was never part of their reality but in mine, they

invaded even my own sleep.

They were the reason why I wanted to be strong,

but I realize they're making me weak.

And I knew I still wanted to keep them despite how

many times they lied,

I was never even this friend that they want to be in

their circle no matter how much I tried.

I will always be an open door while they looked at

me like I was just a bird lost in flight.

Never a part of them, and it was okay for me even

if this friendship is not worth a fight.

WRITTEN ACHES

I remember how it aches at night.

It was something I would usually write.

The ache towered me with its gigantic height.

As I hug my trembling self so tight.

I remember how it aches during the day.

The look I see in the mirror says I have no other way.

It's like the pain when the sun hit my eyes with its rays.

And happiness kept walking away.

The day they left is the day I learned.

Perhaps there were so many aches I need to discern.

Sadness and constantly missing became the only thing I earned.

My broken heart, after all, was never their concern.

I wonder when this pain would stop.

My tears they cease to drop.

My walls keep reaching the top.

I don't know what to do with my emotions when it's mixed-up.

Maybe that's why I woke up for some mornings feeling so damn tired.

And that I knew last night, I gave my best and God knows I've tried.

But why do I always trade myself for people who lied?

Just like them, you left waves on my doorstep, I can't deal with tides.

I knew this chest will only carry nothing but pain.

Blended with names of people and chances that I cannot name.

I know I had no right to dart them, so I pricked myself such blames.

Maybe life's too hopeless and second chances never came.

SLOW PROGRESS

Little by little, I'd like to take a step.

Whatever it may be, I will surely accept.

I want to see what's outside my comfort zone.

I know, I need to see what's on the unknown.

If I need something, then I must work hard.

Learning from something is truly an award.

I must acknowledge all the how's and why's.

I will never know if I'll never try.

Progress may move a little slow.

But I'll dance on rains so it'll help me grow,

It'll make me feel low or maybe a little high.

After all, my self-belief is where I should rely.

I'll fill in my pages with trust.

Bravery is truly a must.

Through adversities, I need to be wise.

I need to begin from the bottom so I'll aim to rise.

If needed so, then maybe I should adjust.

I should never let my dreams be eaten by rust.

I could work hard on nights until the hopes resized.

I need to be optimistic because life is stuffed with surprise.

Small progress is still a progress.

I should just learn while still in the process.

To try is to eradicate the chances of regrets.

I need to keep trying so everything I want —I could get.

HEADING TO FUTURE

Days always move forward.

Some nights might be too hard.

We are not getting any younger.

Our age is more than just numbers.

As we grow up, the demands became louder.

Our minutes are paid, so as our hours.

Days are counted, plans are in order.

But why moments of happiness seemed a little too shorter?

Growing up comes with no brake.

We deal with courage or we deal with ache.

The future sometimes seems far —sometimes it's near.

Sometimes it's blurry and other times it's clear.

Perhaps, growing up means seeing more to life.

It's more than just being okay or being fine.

Growing up means being able to stand after a fall.

It's about wanting to overcome fears; may it be big or small.

Our childhood became a subtle past.

We hope that our memories of it will last.

We might miss it once in a while.

But we had it inside us to remind us to smile.

Hence, the day we're in somehow leads us to the future.

Growing up made us want to live a life that's secure.

We only want to be the bigger person until the end.

We don't want to regret the life that we have and the time that we spent.

JUST ME

As I close the door and dived on the bed.

I acknowledge the questions that I had inside my head.

And these tears, I wonder how many times I should shed.

I can't be better, that's what they said.

I wonder why I can't be better.

I wonder why my turn was taking forever.

I wonder why they're best at any weather.

I was always at the lowest —that's all I could remember.

I toss and turn, shooing all discouragements.

I don't know where my passion went.

Nobody believes in me, failure to me was fated and meant.

I grew tired of lifting my feet; I lost my motivation to the extent.

As I tried to stare at the ceiling longer than I should.

I realized it was me who was never proud of where I stood.

I never believed that I am neither better nor good.

I stopped believing in myself that I could.

So I stopped waiting for the world to lift me up.

I don't want to wait for them to fill in the cup.

I don't want to listen to them if I should fly or jump.

I will ascend and to me, their pending help won't disrupt.

I will build my own solid ground.

I will find my way to make my world go round.

I will create my own music using my own sound.

And I will find my way out —I'll be lost and I'll be found.

THEIR BELIEFS

Do you always believe the words that were freed

from the tip of someone's tongue?

Do you allow these things to hit your soul as it

stung?

Do you permit them to change your fixed plan?

Have they told you to need to listen when you

should walk or run?

Has someone shoved their beliefs right into your

face?

How it troubled you because they forced you to run

on their own phase?

Has it left you baffled and dazed?

And deceived you that they'll help you find your way out of the maze?

Does anyone force you to believe in what they believed?

Have they promised you they won't ever leave?

Have their beliefs controlled you like you're a puppet that cleaved?

Or does it make you uncomfortable because or unrelieved?

Always remember that you are free to listen to your own heart.

You are allowed to draw anything and call it your art.

Believe in yourself because you believed in other parts.

Always take chances to see where you should end and when to start.

It's okay to listen to what seems clear to be heard,

You are allowed to filter their preaches and hypocrite words.

You are permitted to step out of their artificial worlds.

Always listen to your heart until it allows you to see what's no longer blurred.

Their beliefs must be left at the top of the table.

And no force to put it in your pocket when you're unable.

It should be up to you, think if it makes your world

stable.

And through it, appreciation of life is seen and

enabled.

INCONSISTENT REALITY

The walls are high.

The cliffs are sharp.

The worries are loud.

We wonder when we'll die.

The roads are stiff.

The alleys are dark.

The oceans are deep.

We wonder if life too brief.

The books are new.

The tales are old.

The lights were dimmed.

We wonder how much we knew.

The days are short.

The nights are long.

The anguishes expand.

We wonder when we'll get the support.

The people are the same.

The places are unfamiliar

The experiences are bold.

We wonder who'll stay in the game.

The reality is inconsistent.

The old wounds still hurt.

The sadness is temporary.

We wonder who'll remain distant.

BLESSING IN BAD THINGS

I sometimes feel a little lost.

On my bed, I turn and I toss.

My confusion I carried up in the loft.

My happiness seemed to have a cost.

I wonder why I have to watch people leave.

My soft soul has always been deceived.

I had my heart behind my sleeves.

I grew so tired of how I always grieve.

The nights have always been sadder.

Questions left me a little madder.

My worries are there on the scatter.

I wonder if I still matter.

But then again, I wonder about my pain.

Maybe I failed to see the blessings in the rain.

I covered my heart with so much feign.

And allowed history to stain.

Hence, I realize there's something more.

It's a big world outside this door.

There's more to kisses of waves from the shore.

And when it rains, yes it always pours.

Blessings don't only come in good things.

There's more to what we actually think.

Good things emerge from something bad in just a blink.

We could always take failures as a reason to stand after we shrink.

ACHIEVED

Victories became our goals.

Our fate is all we could control.

Satisfaction is what we feed our souls.

We want to make sure to keep up with our roles.

Happiness is all that we aimed.

We want to do things we aren't ashamed.

We want them to remember all of our names.

And fill our voids with certainty with no blames.

For once, we wanted something to accomplish.

We wanted to make things perfectly polished.

We wished all the doubts in our system would

abolish.

And stand grandly like a mountain at its tallest.

Fulfillment means watching yourself in front of a mirror.

Able to see things nearer.

As you listen to your plans, the sound became clearer.

Your dreams became truly bigger.

But to feel fulfillment, you must see the contrary.

You need to feel the failure until you're finally ready.

You'll need to feel sadness to appreciate how it feels to be merry.

You have to experience what's empty before you could have the many.

To fail to is strive for success.

To get stuck makes you want to progress.

You need to feel the silence until you're able to express.

You have to hear their 'no's' until you finally got the yes.

INFIDELITY

It all began with small mistakes.

Silent sneaks and when no one's awake.

And meet there with the moonlit lake.

Infidelity was what they constantly make.

Somehow they knew it was wrong.

They knew it will never last that long.

No matter what they do, they just don't belong.

They only take courage when it's finally dawn.

They tried to shove the truth behind the carpet.

They tried to hide the reality behind their pockets.

Their softness for each other became the only

target.

They knew what will happen; they see it at its

darkest.

As they promised each other their tomorrows,

They didn't know someone's waiting at home —

facing the sorrows.

The time they spend was only borrowed.

And surging pain will surely follow.

It was love but it was also deception.

It was still a sin, no exception.

Both were too afraid of disconnection.

It was a sinful love affair, no need for questions.

They need to stop but they're still too afraid.

Come what may, it'll still rain in their parade.

They knew their unfaithfulness cuts sharper than a blade.

No matter what they do, they can't make love stay.

WRONG AND WRITE

What makes something bad?

Was it remorse, or feeling a little sad?

Was it being ungrateful for the things I had?

Was it hurting back people when you're mad?

What makes something good?

Was it bravery to find your way out of the woods?

Was it making sure you secure where you stood?

Was it lifting someone as you tell them they could?

What makes something incorrect?

Was it pursuing something without being checked?

Was it answering back out of disrespect?

Was it making sure they listen as you object?

What makes something proper?

Was it writing everything correctly in the next chapter?

Was it leaning back no matter how you get further?

Was it assuring nobody gets hurt from your daggers?

What makes something wrong?

Was it choosing the weak ones over those who are strong?

Was it leading someone somewhere until they get lost all along?

Was it breaking them until they finally withdraw?

What makes something right?

Was it deleting all the blacks until you're left with white?

Was it purity that remains when you write?

Was it making sure you win all your righteous fights?

STILL MAKING MY WAY TO IT

And I told myself I'll keep going.

No matter how rough, I'll keep growing.

As the waves have gone mad, I'll keep rowing.

In my darkest nights, I'll keep glowing.

And I told myself, I'll keep trying.

In my down moments, I'll keep rising.

When I'm misplaced, I'll keep flying.

My tears, they'll keep drying.

And I told myself, I'll keep fighting.

The battles I am facing; I am no longer hiding.

My frustrations, I'll keep writing.

In this crazy life, I'll keep riding.

And I told myself, I'll keep dancing.

Along with my shadow, no longer passing.

I will my troubles, no more running.

I'll sway with it; my walls are no longer collapsing.

And I told myself, I'll keep singing.

In life's challenges, I'll keep swinging.

My positive reminders will keep ringing.

I believe this is yet the beginning.

And I told myself, I'll keep searching.

My future, I swear I won't be worrying.

In every passing moment, chances I'll be seeing.

I promise to one day have what I am seeking.

STRONG FAITH

I live for this salvation.

All these endless repent.

So as my strong beliefs.

God sees me with his clear vision.

The days walk in a span.

The sinners feel sorrow.

The forgivers feel at ease.

He gave us feelings to become a man.

Satan remains to tease.

But faith towers.

Fears could be overcome.

We will surpass all of these.

We will be saved by our faith.

As we stumble and as we fall.

We'll learn to be brave.

We have no reasons to be afraid.

Life holds mysteries.

May we understand errors.

May we learn from mistakes.

May we daze these miseries.

To God may we surrender our trust.

Surrender our sins.

Surrender our weaknesses.

Before our bodies turn into dust.

IN NEED OF DISCIPLINE

She's hard to tame.

She set her own rules.

She had her own games to play.

And from the rest, she's not the same.

She smokes cigs every now and then.

She didn't care about what you say.

Unlike anyone, she's recklessly untamed.

Her mistakes, she did it once again.

She wonders who truly cares.

Nobody bravely steps toe on her line.

Everyone's afraid, nobody dares.

She's tough, especially when she stares.

Then entered her room alone.

She cried until she fell tired.

Nobody's there on her side.

After all, she's still on her own.

She needs someone to tell her to stop.

She needed someone to tell her what's wrong and right.

Especially on her vulnerable nights.

She hoped someone would pull her from the top.

To be tamed is all she wanted.

She's freer than birds, she said.

Still the young, sad, undisciplined.

After all, she's incessantly haunted.

THE CONSTANT HARD TIMES

How do we live in this sinful world?

Where everyone only sees the errors on my codes?

As well as when our heart turned suddenly cold.

When we're astray, which do you think is the right road?

Sometimes I wonder how far I could go.

I just want to leave; all these bad memories I want to throw.

For I had always been at the least —always at the low.

Perhaps, I don't know what this life is trying to show.

Do problems exist so hope can vanish?

Was it there to emphasize what I can't manage?

Does vintage heartache linger to remind me of its damage?

And so I could carry it like heavy baggage?

As I walk my way out, I didn't know what to do.

I keep losing track of these places that have the same view.

Maybe I was here just to leave in grey and blue.

Life never failed to break my heart into two.

I wonder how long will I endure.

All these pains look like it has no cure.

I lost all energy, I am no longer sure.

My sun never showed up, my rain clouds always obscure.

As I walk, I was going nowhere.

I lost all solutions, nobody seemed to care.

They see my trouble, everyone's completely aware.

But seems like nobody's willing to save me from this despair.

AFTER THE FALL

I was able to arise; I was able to breathe.

I was given another chance to believe.

I knew life after all is brief.

This time, I look forward to achieve.

I was able to restore; I was able to stand.

I was given a chance to step foot on my land,

I knew life is tough, I just need to understand.

The next time I fall, I'll make sure it'll be on the sand.

I was able to regain. I was able to run.

I was given a chance to chase the fun.

Unfinished things will soon be done.

I will start again for a new life has begun.

I was able to nurture; I was able to fly.

I was given another chance to get by.

I'll bring my dreams to the highest highs.

I will make sure that I'll never stop to try.

I was able to accept; I was able to learn

I was given another chance to discern.

The world was cruel and always stern.

But I'll make sure in every try, I have something to earn.

I was able to rest; I was able to pause.

I was given another chance to hear the applause.

The world is contradicting and filled with flaws.

I'll learn to pick myself up whenever I fall.

TO THE STRONGEST PEOPLE I KNOW

Mother, you always wake up earlier than you should.

You always make sure the breakfast is served.

You warmed the water for me even though I could.

You put me first, always making sure I am heard.

Father, you taught me what true love is,

Thank you for showing me the best that you have.

On little things, happiness is enough.

You trained me to be brave when life turns rough.

Mother, when were little you had some good stories to tell.

You make sure I'm in good health and only decent memories could dwell.

You deserve everything and that's why we always wish you well.

Thank you for the guidance until I learned how to come out from my shell.

Father, I will one day grant you the best of everything.

I wish you nothing but just a blessed life that clings.

I will always look back to how you built us until we had our own wings.

Someday, it'll be my turn to give back the care that you always bring

Mother, ever since I was a kid, you answered my whys and hows.

And opened so many windows when I needed it now.

You always flood me with compliments and things I deserve to know.

And you raised me so well; you've stayed with me as I grow.

Father, I'd like to give you your happiest day.

Leave all the worries and take the best along the way.

Be in love with life and forget about the chapters that are grey.

You two became my heroes, the only people who took all my insecurities away.

LET'S GO

Let's go into the unknown.

Let's go where the winds blow.

Let's go where there's no signal on our phones.

Let's go where the sun always shows.

Let's go where there are seashells and stones.

Let's go where happiness doesn't postpone.

Let's go where others are unaware of its time zone.

Let's go where we could forget that we're alone.

Let's go where paper cities look thin below.

Let's go where the currents of the river calmly flow.

Let's go where stars always aglow.

And coldness seemed like it's about to snow.

Let's go to places nobody has ever been.

Let's go to the new cliffs where it has a breathtaking scene.

Let's go where happiness comes free and not mean.

Let's go where oceans blend our favorite blue jeans.

Let's go where trees and grass turn a little more green.

Let's go where the air we breathe is truly clean.

Let's go and chase sunset like we were only sixteen.

Let's go where sadness will no longer intervene.

Let's go to where silence heals what we break.

Let's go where memories are free to make.

Let's go where the moon reflects on the lake.

Let's go to these places where we're all allowed to make mistakes.

OUT SOMEWHERE

Wake up early and pack your bags.

And those who want to come could always tag.

Prepare for the buckles and zig zags.

We'll go somewhere as time drags,

For months, we always come out with plans.

We'll take courage and make things on hand.

We'll only take the exciting ones, and we'll leave the bland.

We'll bring the best on the land where we stand.

We'll stay for a few nights.

We'll visit beautiful sites.

We'll taste the greatest delights.

And rewrite memories that bring us light.

We'll bring summer in October.

We'll enjoy it like it won't be over.

We'll ask sunlight to come closer.

And wish for time to move slower.

We'll forget for a while.

We'll travel hundreds of miles.

We will give ourselves more reasons to smile.

And take the greatest risks on spotted trials.

We should talk for a walk as we talk under the sun.

I swear, this won't be the last —it'll never be counted and done.

We'll take every morning for fun as we run.

Adventure awaits, the fuel of optimism began.

VANISH FOR A WHILE

When you want to run, where do you go?

When you want to be alone, what do you do?

When you want to rest, what is your favorite view?

When you say friends, can you at least name a few?

When you want to escape, which place?

When you want to recall happiness, whose face?

When you want to dance, what song you play with

grace?

When you want to forget, who do you need to

replace?

When you want to walk away, which steps would

you trace?

When you think of a sunset, when will you chase?

When you feel like you're falling apart, who do you want to embrace?

When you want peace, who would you share that space?

When you want to let go, who would you forget?

When you want to start again, what plan would your set?

When you want to restart, to whom would you pay the debts?

When you want to move on, which memory did you regret?

When you want to travel, how long would it be?

When you want to calm down, would you prefer dipping in the sea?

When you want to renew, does it mean you have to be free?

When you want to give in, would they agree that you'll disagree?

When you want to leave, would you imagine yourself going somewhere?

When you want to disappear, who do you think would still care?

When you want to come back, who would reserve you a chair?

When you want to escape, would you understand that life is never fair?

SUSTAINING SUCCESS

After so many times of trying, I finally made it.

I was able to find corners where my potentials fit.

There I was able to find stability to commit.

And I am contented; I have no reason to quit.

Success smelled like freshwater.

It sometimes sounded like a line written by your favorite author.

It makes me see what's down below the water.

And that alone made me stronger.

Success is the reason why I still want to try.

I knew I could surpass all the troubles that are passing by.

It's like the stars that blink in my night sky.

And that I still crave for more, that something I won't deny.

I will still give my best in everything I do.

I will continue embroiling new dreams I want to pursue.

I will learn from all the mistakes in the past that I can't undo.

For success should be maintained, I must keep it through.

I will continue uncovering some of my hidden skills.

I will never let my dreams die when the sunk silk behind the hill.

I will always search for spaces I could still fill.

I will create my own faith as the crowd stands still.

Despite how far I have gone through, I am still amazed.

I still consider my future as something I'd still gaze.

I'll keep trying despite how the roads are covered with haze.

I knew successes will always my darks phase into better days.

AS ONE

Let's work hand and hand.

Let's discuss what we need to understand.

Together, we will create a plan.

Together, we will make things grand.

Let's work with coherence.

We will teach each other about perseverance.

Together, we will create a difference.

Together, we will reminisce.

Let's work as one.

We have fought the same battle and won.

Together, we will have fun.

Together, we're in this run.

Let's work happily.

We will treat each other as family.

Together, we will face the reality.

Together, we will unfold each other's capacity.

Let's work as a group.

We'll fuel each there with hope.

Together, we will clear the smoke.

Together, we will forger we were broke.

Let's work as a team.

We'll figure our life's daily theme.

Together, we will dream.

Together, we will regain our self-esteem.

THE WORLD OUT THERE

You deserve sunshine,

You deserve a break.

You deserve an old wine.

You deserve a sight of the lake.

You deserve to travel.

You deserve a breather.

You deserve moments to unravel.

You deserve perfect weather.

You deserve a hike.

You deserve a ride on a bike.

You deserve to travel to where you like.

You deserve to go where daylight strikes.

You deserve a hotel night.

You deserve a place that's quiet.

You deserve to book a flight.

You deserve views that fade your fright.

You deserve to be on the shore.

You deserve adventures that call for more.

You deserve walks in the afternoon at four.

You deserve waves that roar.

You deserve bliss.

You deserve the sun's kiss.

You deserve to get found in the abyss.

You deserve a grant in your wish.

SOME THINGS

Some days might be darker.

Some waves cling to anger.

Some plans lost their order.

Some pain might ache sharper.

Some songs might be unheard.

Some sights might be blurred.

Some words might be slurred.

Some cuts come uncured.

Some worries won't go away.

Some roads will lead you astray.

Some happiness won't last a day.

Some clouds turn a little gray.

Some ghost still visits.

Some dreams don't appear vivid.

Some bliss lasts only for a minute.

Some excitements have their limits.

Some poems lost their rhymes.

Some love doesn't last a lifetime.

Some dreams weren't written on lines.

Some evening, you'll forget you're fine.

Some days aren't perfect.

Some rights are not checked.

Some promises weren't kept.

Some challenges will keep you upset.

SLOW PROGRESS

It all started small,

Like baby steps on empty halls.

I knew I won't have it all,

But I could make my dreams tall.

It started simple,

Like the wind that whistles.

I knew I must stay longer in the middle,

But I have fires that I want to kindle.

It all started as a vision,

Like the unuttered mission.

As I planned all my decisions,

My motivation and positivity went on collision.

It all started as a reverie,

Like a visualization that formed cleverly.

As I solely inject them in my memory,

I also need to clutch bravery.

It all started as a tiny hope.

Like wishing, I could reach the end of the rope.

There were corners I had been in my scope.

But I see opportunities like a kaleidoscope.

It all started as a trance,

Now I have it in my hands.

Progression works if you demand.

Do not be afraid to fall in sands.

ACCEPTING WHAT WE CAN'T CHANGE

I realized there are things I can't change.

There'll be familiar things that would turn strange.

Some things happen in a suddenly altered range.

And life will turn messy or disarranged.

I learned that people don't always stay.

They leave when they bend and sway.

Something their reasons we can't weigh.

But we have no choice but to watch them walk away.

There'll be times where we didn't know why it has to happen.

The way they hold you will slowly unfasten.

And I found no reason to try or keep laughing.

We just watch them while heartache keeps passing.

That's when I thought my heart to forgive.

To forgive is to forget that will soon help you relive.

I get to accept that I'll lose something if I give.

And I'll learn to get used to the lost trust like loosen weave.

We learn to understand so we could accept.

That everyone who came became the ones we can't keep.

We watched life take them away like dreams in our sleep.

And heal the touches they left turn into cuts.

To teach your heart how to accept is not easy.

You can't insist on it when your heart's still busy.

You need to clear your mind when it's still too hazy.

So you could learn to love freely.

SAME GROUNDS

May we all see the world through the same lens.

Where we get to be surrounded by real friends.

Where chances provided won't come to an end.

Where equality gives everyone a chance to ascend.

As the world continues to revolve,

I pray everyone gets involved.

And believe that every problem could be resolved.

And make a change as it evolves.

May discriminations stop standing like a hindrance.

May opportunities might be based on appearance.

It should be based on skills and perseverance.

And make this a better place for an instance.

May we all be treated fairly.

May we receive parts squarely.

May we get used to a setting that's friendly.

And to make this a better world for everyone sparely.

We should look on the inside.

May we all uncover what we hide.

May we all sway to the unpredictable tide

And grant those as they stride.

Equality is essential.

It unleashes hidden potentials.

It reaches all the dimensions.

And every hope that most of us can't mention.

CHEERS

Cheers to the good times.

Pour in the glass your red wine.

And burst the laughter with a rhyme.

And say you're feeling high and prime.

Cheers for the conquest.

Recall how you did your best.

The victory calls for a feast.

As the sun sunk in the west.

Cheers for passing,

This night, we'll be dancing.

We'll make this moment long-lasting.

While the cameras are flashing.

Cheers for surviving.

Another success is thriving.

This indeed perfect timing.

As your motivation keeps uprising.

Cheers for another day.

You just find another solution and way.

You dared to finally say.

And overcome how doubts used to play.

Cheers for another achievement.

This is what your fate truly meant.

Inhale joy like nature's scent.

And live in the moment to the full extent.

THROUGH GOOD OR BAD TIMES

I always thought that you were this someone I'll

never grow to heart to love.

We didn't have a memory to remember about the

things we shared and the things we had.

Its funny how we didn't meet halfway, I was down

while you were above.

And right from that moment, I knew friendship

between us will never arrive.

You were this person I hadn't been so close and we

never walked at the same speed.

I was always out of line and never knew what

languages you speak.

I thought you were this someone who's too distant and rejects people who were weak.

And maybe that's why I never opened myself to the kindle of friendship, not even in my sleep.

But fate always has its ways, to make people be friends especially those with the same blood.

You made me realize you're not even bad.

You stayed with me when I had problems and nights I cried a flood.

You showed to me an amazing sight towards the capability of my heart to thud.

Thank you so much for being good company; you will always be my favorite aunt.

You always stay with me telling me you're willing to

listen to all of my rants.

You always know my softest parts and days where

all I could ever say are "no's" and "can't's"

You always tend to teach me to battle my fears and

never stop my lines in "but's".

I wish you a happy life, to stay brave and the

realities of your plan.

You deserve everything, every little crumb of

adventure and fun.

And the best of everything in every path you take

in your long run.

Believe in yourself because we believe in you, we

know you can.

And thank you for the friendship that showed me

what truly is love.

You disclosed to me that having real people is

worth to keep and have.

You stood by me no matter what the weather, no

matter how rough.

I didn't need a huge circle of friends; your sincerity

is enough.

LIFE LESSONS

You will one day realize all the things that you still don't have.

Including the ones you truly love.

In your corners, you never wanted to get out.

You had been swallowed by fear and doubt.

You want to understand the beating of your heart,

In all the poems and poetry, and on art.

In a world full of inconsistencies, you just need to calm.

And keep modesty within your palm.

You then realized that some things have a limit.

While others fade after they commit.

It will break you or shatter you, that's something you admit.

But you put yourself back like puzzles that fit.

But then, you learn to appreciate the day and the sunshine.

You start to hope that everything will soon be fine.

You said it's sometimes okay to play blind.

And keep unnecessary anger inside your mind.

You learn to let go of all the unsaid signs.

And will still love and choose to remain kind.

May it be on days where your mornings start at nine,

And start enjoying your own company when you dine.

You stopped waiting to have someone to lean.

Not all people could walk on your paved lane.

You knew that rains are normal behind the windowpane.

And started hoping nobody remembers your name.

You started seeing the purpose of why you need to fight.

You stopped waiting for someone to be your knight.

You found comfort even in your silent night.

And learn to keep yourself together uptight.

RUMORS FLY

There, she saw how rumors fly.

Out of all the people, she asks why.

At night, all she ever does is cry.

She did her best, she gave it a try.

There, she saw how rumors fly.

People talk behind her back, it was wry.

She then started talking to the stars in the sky.

She was left with no one to rely.

There, she saw how rumors fly.

It all started in July.

She lost all her friends from nearby.

She just wanted to play a blind eye.

There, she saw how rumors fly.

She realized the world is hard to satisfy.

In their standards, she was not qualified.

Sadness consumed her, it always intensifies.

There, she saw how rumors fly.

She wanted to be herself, she can't magnify.

Problems she can't identify.

Her true sexuality will never hide nor die.

There, she saw how rumors fly.

And this time, she will never lie.

Gossips spread, but she'll get by,

Opinions of the other, she won't buy,

VERSUS

Black versus white,

Dark versus light.

Battles are subconsciously tight,

Nobody wants to lose the fight.

Good versus bad.

Satisfied versus mad.

Comparisons that they had

Were the reason why there weren't glad.

Happiness versus sadness.

Hollow versus vastness,

There are tears wiped on a mattress.

It separates the world from its axis.

Compare versus contrast.

Fear versus trust.

Some things were not discussed.

But we hope fate will learn to adjust.

Fondness versus disgust.

Rightness versus unjust.

Competence was eaten by rust.

Acceptance should be a must.

Gloomy versus sunny.

Clarity versus blurry.

Differences hit in a hurry.

We find ourselves along with the many.

WHO IS MA. CARINA DIZON?

Ma. Carina Catubay Dizon is an educator, musician, and writer. She holds her Bachelors Degree in Education Major in English and currently a Candidate for the degree of Master of Arts in English Language and Literature Teaching, still on her Thesis. In the year 2010 she published her book entitled "The Cute Girl and Handsome Guy."

In the year 2017, she already have her own website www.carinadizonmaellt.com and in the year 2020, she finish four short courses in TESDA, Orienting oneself to Environmentally Sustainable work Standards, Exercising Sustainable Development in the Workplace, Receiving and Responding to Workplace Communication, and Plan Training Session.

She also got her Certificate in Web Designing using HTML 5, CSS 3, Bootstrap, and Graphic Design101, conducted by the Department of Information Communication Technology, (DICT) where she was able to showcase her own website.

Also, she completed "The Policy Forum Series on Decentralization, Constitutional Reform, and Governance Innovations during COVID -19 Pandemic" conducted by the Department of the Interior and Local Government (DILG)

Facebook: @Ma. Carina C. Dizon

              @Inspired Carina

Website: www.carinadizonmaellt.com

E-Mail: carinadizon916@gmail.com

OTHER BOOKS BY EDISON DIZON

SHADES OF SEASONS: Soulful Autumn

SHADES OF SEASONS: Cold Dark Winter's Night

SHADES OF SEASONS: Endless Spring

SHADES OF SEASONS: Summertime Blues

ISANG TASA NG TSAA PARA SA'YO: Tula at Prosa

THE VOICE WITHIN MY SOUL

TAG-ULAN SA KAARAWAN NI JUAN: Dagli at

Maikling Kwento

THE SOUL SENTIMENTS: LIKE LAST NIGHT NEVER

HAPPENED

TWILIT HORIZON: SENTIMENTS OF THE SEASONS